OVER
IN THE MEADOW

OVER
IN THE MEADOW

PUFFIN BOOKS

illustrated by EZRA JACK KEATS

PUFFIN BOOKS
Published by the Penguin Group
Penguin Putnam Books for Young Readers, 345 Hudson Street, New York, New York 10014, U.S.A.
Penguin Books Ltd, 27 Wrights Lane, London W8 5TZ, England
Penguin Books Australia Ltd, Ringwood, Victoria, Australia
Penguin Books Canada Ltd, 10 Alcorn Avenue, Toronto, Ontario, Canada M4V 3B2
Penguin Books (N.Z.) Ltd, 182-190 Wairau Road, Auckland 10, New Zealand

Penguin Books Ltd, Registered Offices: Harmondsworth, Middlesex, England

First published in the United States of America by Four Winds Press, a Division of Scholastic Magazines, Inc., 1971
Published by Viking and Puffin Books, members of Penguin Putnam Books for Young Readers, 1999

39 40 38

Illustrations copyright © Ezra Jack Keats, 1971
Illustrations copyright renewed Martin Pope, Executor of the Estate of Ezra Jack Keats, 1999
Illustrations copyright assigned to Ezra Jack Keats Foundation
All rights reserved

LIBRARY OF CONGRESS CATALOGING-IN-PUBLICATION DATA
Keats, Ezra Jack.
Over in the meadow / by Ezra Jack Keats.
p.   cm.
Summary: An old nursery poem introduces animals and their young
and the numbers one through ten.
ISBN 978-0-670-88344-8.— ISBN 978-0-14-056508-9 (pbk.)
1. Nursery rhymes. 2. Children's poetry. [1. Nursery rhymes.
2. Animals—Poetry. 3. Counting.] I. Title
PZ8.3.K227Ov 1999 [E]—dc21 98-47037 CIP AC

Manufactured in China

The text for *Over in the Meadow* is based on the original version attributed to Olive A. Wadsworth.

To Bernice

Over in the meadow, in the sand, in the sun,
Lived an old mother turtle and her little turtle one.

"Dig!" said the mother.
"I dig," said the one.
So he dug all day,
In the sand, in the sun.

Over in the meadow, where the stream runs blue,
Lived an old mother fish and her little fishes two.

"Swim!" said the mother.
"We swim," said the two.
 So they swam and they leaped,
 Where the stream runs blue.

Over in the meadow, in a hole in a tree,
Lived a mother bluebird and her little birdies three.

"Sing!" said the mother.
"We sing," said the three.
So they sang and were glad,
In the hole in the tree.

Over in the meadow, in the reeds on the shore,
Lived a mother muskrat and her little ratties four.

"Dive!" said the mother.
"We dive," said the four.
  So they dived and they burrowed,
  In the reeds on the shore.

Over in the meadow, in a snug beehive,
Lived a mother honeybee and her little honeys five.

"Buzz!" said the mother.
"We buzz," said the five.
  So they buzzed and they hummed,
  Near the snug beehive.

Over in the meadow, in a nest built of sticks,
Lived a black mother crow and her little crows six.

"Caw!" said the mother.
"We caw," said the six.
So they cawed and they called,
In their nest built of sticks.

Over in the meadow, where the grass is so even,
Lived a gay mother cricket and her little crickets seven.

"Chirp!" said the mother.
"We chirp," said the seven.
So they chirped cheery notes,
In the grass soft and even.

Over in the meadow, by the old mossy gate,
Lived a brown mother lizard and her little lizards eight.

"Bask!" said the mother.
"We bask," said the eight.
So they basked in the sun,
By the old mossy gate.

Over in the meadow, where the clear pools shine,
Lived a green mother frog and her little froggies nine.

"Croak!" said the mother.
"We croak," said the nine.
So they croaked and they jumped,
Where the clear pools shine.

Over in the meadow, in a soft shady glen,
Lived a mother firefly and her little flies ten.

"Shine!" said the mother.
"We shine," said the ten.
So they shone like stars,
In the soft shady glen.

Also by Ezra Jack Keats

Apt. 3
Goggles!
A Letter to Amy
My Dog Is Lost
Peter's Chair
The Snowy Day
Whistle for Willie